cl♣verleaf books™

Our American Symbols

Why Is the Statue of Liberty Green?

Martha E. H. Rustad

illustrated by **Holli Conger**

M MILLBROOK PRESS · MINNEAPOLIS

For my sisters, who encouraged me to climb
to the top —M.E.H.R.

For W.C. and O.C.—looking forward to our
history adventures together! —H.C.

Millbrook Press
A division of Lerner Publishing Group, Inc.
241 First Avenue North
Minneapolis, MN 55401 USA

For reading levels and more information, look up this title at
www.lernerbooks.com.

Images in this book used with the permission of : © Luciano Mortula/
Shutterstock.com, p. 23.

Main body text set in Slappy Inline 18/28.
Typeface provided by T26.

Library of Congress Cataloging-in-Publication Data

Rustad, Martha E. H. (Martha Elizabeth Hillman), 1975–
    Why Is the Statue of Liberty Green? / by Martha E. H. Rustad;
  illustrated by Holli Conger
        pages   cm. — (Cloverleaf Books™ — American Symbols)
    Includes index.
    ISBN 978–1–4677–2139–4 (lib. bdg. : alk. paper)
    ISBN 978–1–4677–4774–5 (eBook)
    1. Statue of Liberty (New York, N.Y.)—Juvenile literature. 2. New York
(N.Y.)—Buildings, structures, etc.—Juvenile literature. I. Conger, Holli,
illustrator. II. Title.
F128.64.L6R87 2015
974.7'1—dc23   2013034227

Manufactured in the United States of America
1 – BP – 7/15/14

TABLE OF CONTENTS

Chapter One

A Visit to the Statue of Liberty

Our class is going on a **field trip!**
Mrs. Bolt makes us guess where.

"What's green and as tall as a twenty-two-story building?" she asks.

"A dinosaur!" shouts Elijah.

"A green skyscraper!" guesses Elizabeth.

"We're going to visit the **Statue of Liberty**," Mrs. Bolt says.

"What does *liberty* mean?" Kiara asks.

Mrs. Bolt answers, "***Liberty* means 'freedom.'**"

Statue of Liberty

The Statue of Liberty stands in New York Harbor. Smaller copies of the statue stand in cities around the world, from Paris, France, to Buenos Aires, Argentina, to Fargo, North Dakota.

We take a ferry to **Liberty Island**. We meet Ranger Alisha at the flagpole. She teaches visitors about the monument.

"The Statue of Liberty was a **gift** from France to the United States," she tells us. "It was a **symbol** of **friendship**. Workers in France spent nine years building it."

"A gift?" asks Ali. "How would you wrap a present that big?"

Ranger Alisha says workers took the statue apart and put it in it 214 boxes! A ship carried the boxes to New York in 1885.

A symbol is something that stands for something else. The Statue of Liberty stands for freedom.

We walk to the front of the **Statue of Liberty.** The statue sits on a huge base. Ranger Alisha calls it the **pedestal.**

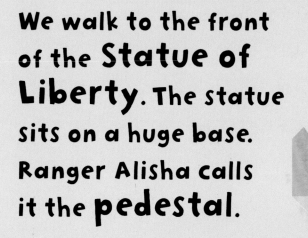

The pedestal is 154 feet (47 meters) tall. The statue is 151 feet (46 m) tall. Together, they are 305 feet (93 m) tall. That is as long as three football fields!

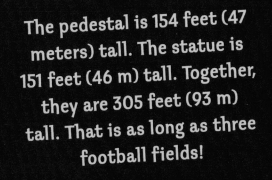

We learn that American workers built the base. "A woman named **Emma Lazarus** wrote a poem about the Statue of Liberty," Ranger Alisha says. "Her poem inspired thousands of Americans to donate money to build the pedestal."

Then workers put the statue back together on the base. **The Statue of Liberty opened to visitors in 1886.**

Chapter Two

Inside the Pedestal

Next, we go inside the pedestal. It's like a museum.

"Oh, no!" says Ella. "Did the **torch** fall down?"

Ranger Alisha says this is the old torch. Workers put up a new torch.

She says the new **flame** is covered in **real gold**. Lights reflect off the shiny surface.

At night, the flame can be seen out at sea from as far as 12 miles (19 kilometers) away.

We look at a copy of the statue's face.
The nose is taller than we are!

"The Statue of Liberty is made of
copper, like a **penny**," Ranger
Alisha tells us.

"But pennies are brown," says Maria. "The statue looks green."

"Right!" says Ranger Alisha. "The statue was coppery brown when it was new. Rain, wind, and the sun slowly changed the color to green."

The green layer is called a patina. It forms when copper mixes with water and changes into a mineral called malachite.

Chapter Three

The Big Climb

Time to go up the stairs! We climb up **156 steps** to the top of the pedestal. "My legs are so tired!" says Tony.

Sculptor Frédéric-Auguste Bartholdi designed the statue. A man named Gustave Eiffel built the frame. He is famous for building the Eiffel Tower in Paris.

We look up—way up—inside the statue. "You can see the steel frame," points out Ranger Alisha. "The frame is kind of like Lady Liberty's bones. It holds her up."

Let's go outside!
"I can see **New York City!**"
Michael shouts.

The statue's full name
is Liberty Enlightening
the World. People also
call it Lady Liberty.

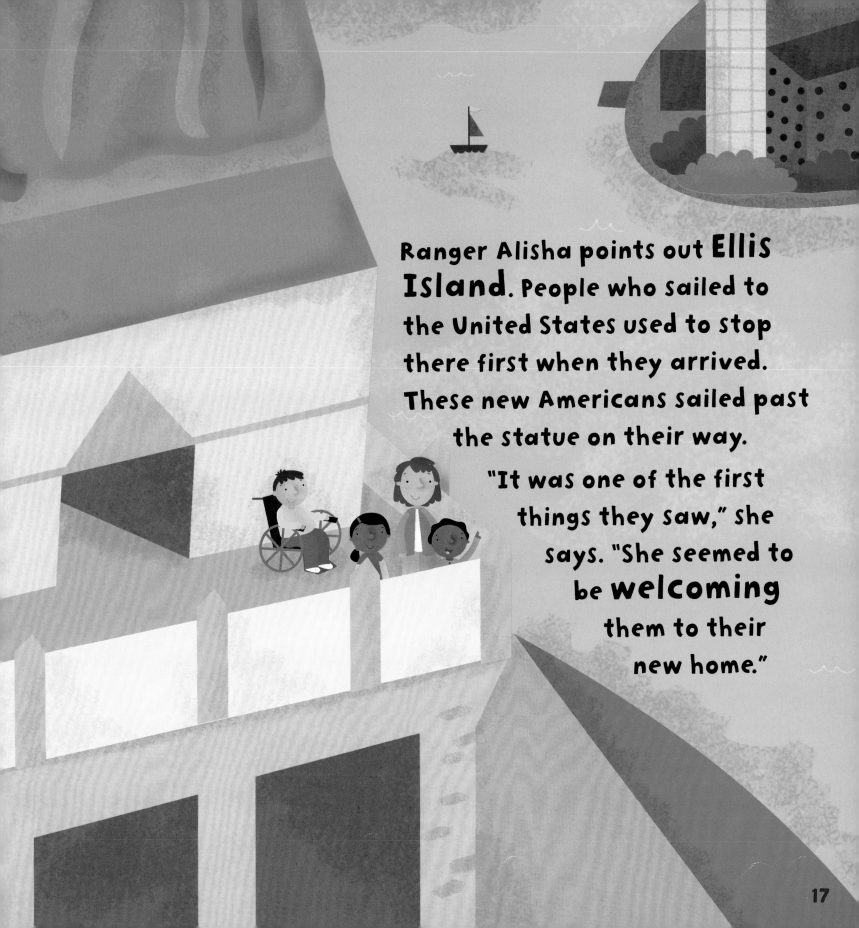

Ranger Alisha points out **Ellis Island.** People who sailed to the United States used to stop there first when they arrived. These new Americans sailed past the statue on their way.

"It was one of the first things they saw," she says. "She seemed to be **welcoming** them to their new home."

"Can we go up to the **crown**?" Markus asks.

"Not this time," says Mrs. Bolt. "Visitors to the crown need **special tickets**."

Andrea says, "My cousin went up to the crown. She said she was as high as the clouds!"

Ranger Alisha says there are 377 spiral steps up. And down again!

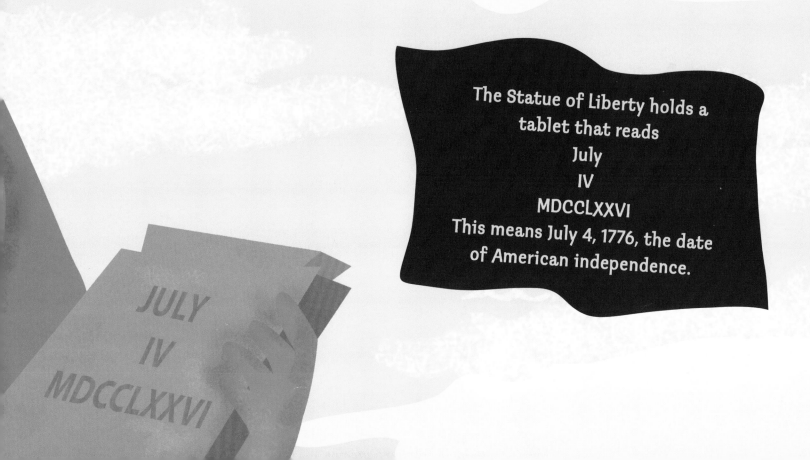

The Statue of Liberty holds a tablet that reads
July
IV
MDCCLXXVI
This means July 4, 1776, the date of American independence.

We climb back down the steps. Our field trip is almost done.

"What do we tell Ranger Alisha?" Mrs. Bolt asks.

"Thank you, Ranger Alisha!" we shout.

As we sail away, Mrs. Bolt says, "The Statue of Liberty is a **Symbol** of **freedom**.

What does freedom mean to you?"

"Going to the park without my brother!" says Sarah.

"Eating whatever kind of ice cream I want!" Tim says.

On the way home, we stop for ice cream. We hold up our cones, just like **Lady Liberty's** torch.

About 3.5 million people visit the Statue of Liberty every year.

Turn Pennies Green

The Statue of Liberty is made of copper. When it was new, it was the color of a penny. Weather caused its green layer to form over time. You can change pennies to match the Statue of Liberty.

What You Need:

glass or plastic bowl

½ cup vinegar

2 teaspoons salt

plastic or wooden spoon

several pennies

paper towels

1) Mix the vinegar and salt in the bowl with the spoon.

2) Put the pennies in the bowl. Let them sit for ten minutes.

3) Use the spoon to take out the pennies. Place them on a paper towel to dry.

4) Check the pennies after an hour.

The green layer that forms on the pennies is called a patina.

GLOSSARY

copper: a reddish-brown metal

liberty: freedom

monument: a statue or building that honors a person or event

patina: a green layer that collects on the surface of copper or bronze

pedestal: a base under a statue

reflect: to shine back light that hits a surface

spiral: winding in a curve

symbol: something that stands for something else

tablet: a flat piece of stone

The Statue of Liberty stands tall on Liberty Island.

BOOKS

Glaser, Linda. *Emma's Poem.* New York: Houghton Mifflin Books for Children, 2010. Paintings by Claire A. Nivola help tell the story of Emma Lazarus and "The New Colossus," the famous poem she wrote that raised money to finish the Statue of Liberty's pedestal.

Moriarty, Siobhan. *Visit the Statue of Liberty.* New York: Gareth Stevens, 2012. Read about a visit to Lady Liberty and look at lots of photographs of the statue.

Staton, Hilarie. *The Statue of Liberty.* New York: Chelsea Clubhouse, 2010. Find out more about the Statue of Liberty.

WEBSITES

Statue of Liberty
http://www.brainpopjr.com/socialstudies/citizenship/statueofliberty/
Watch a short movie about the Statue of Liberty.

Statue of Liberty Replicas
http://www.cheyennetroop101.org/liberty/
Find out where you can see a copy of Lady Liberty.

Statue of Liberty Virtual Tour
http://www.nps.gov/stli/photosmultimedia/virtualtour.htm
Go inside the Statue of Liberty in this National Park Service tour.

LERNER SOURCE™
Expand learning beyond the printed book. Download free, complementary educational resources for this book from our website, www.lerneresource.com.